Also by K. I. Knight

Fate & Freedom — Book I: The Middle Passage

Fate & Freedom — Book II: The Turning Tides

Fate & Freedom — Book III: On Troubled Shores

Unveiled — The Twenty & Odd.
Documenting the First Africans in England's America
1619-1625 and Beyond.

Also by Jane R. Wood

Voices in St. Augustine

Adventures on Amelia Island:
A Pirate, A Princess, and Buried Treasure

Trouble on the St. Johns River

Ghosts on the Coast:
A Visit to Savannah and the Low Country

Lost in Boston

K. I. Knight   Jane R. Wood

Melting Pot Press, LLC.   ◆   Jacksonville, FL

Publisher's Cataloging-In-Publication Data
(Prepared by The Donohue Group, Inc.)

Names: Knight, K. I., author. | Wood, Jane R., 1947- author.
Title: Finding family treasure / K.I. Knight [and] Jane R. Wood.
Description: Jacksonville, FL : Melting Pot Press, LLC., [2022] | Series: [Melting pot kids club] ; [1] | Interest age level: 008-012. | Summary: "'Who are we?' Ms. Johansson asks her class of fifth graders. Her perplexed students soon discover the lesson she wants them to learn. While studying the founding of their country, the class is challenged to understand the melting pot that makes up the American people—both past and present"—Provided by publisher.
Identifiers: ISBN 9781737337102 (paperback) | ISBN 9781737337119 (ebook)
Subjects: LCSH: Multiculturalism—United States—Juvenile fiction. | Genealogy—Juvenile fiction. | United States—History--Juvenile fiction.
Classification: LCC PZ7.1.K659 Fi 2022 (print) | LCC PZ7.1.K659 (ebook) | DDC [Fic]—dc23

Library of Congress Control Number: 2021941847

Cover Design: Mike Woodcock

Published through:

Melting Pot Press, LLC.
11802 Magnolia Falls Drive
Jacksonville, FL 32258
904-268-9572

www.findingfamilytreasure.com

Printed and bound in the USA.

To the next generation of Americans, our young people,

who will join the melting pot of people, past and present,

who make up the United States of America.

Chapter 1 – Who's a Loser?

One minute they were playing a game on Xbox, and the next minute his best friend was calling him a loser.

"Hey, dude, it's only a game," Mike said. "*You're* being a poor loser!"

"No, *you're* the loser," Robbie said. "You don't even know who your real parents are!"

Mike was so stunned he could not speak. That was a mean thing to say, even though it was true. Mike had always known he was adopted, and it had never seemed to matter. Now Robbie's comment made him feel strange.

Mike's mom walked into the room and told Robbie she thought it was time for him to go. She gave Mike a sympathetic look while gesturing Robbie toward the door.

Robbie grabbed up his backpack and left in a huff.

Mike's mom turned off the TV and sat on the floor next to Mike.

"That was a mean thing for Robbie to say," she said. "Do you want to talk about it?"

Mike was quiet for a moment. His head was bowed and his hands were clenched into fists.

"No, I'm fine."

"You know the fact that you're adopted does not make you a loser. You're as much a member of this family as Danny and Sarah, and we love you."

"I know. It's just that I didn't know other people knew, and thought of me as different," he said. "I know being Black makes me different from Robbie, but I guess he thinks I'm weird because I'm adopted."

Mike watched his mother's face during a long silence while she searched for the right words to say. She knew this day would come. She herself had experienced it.

She had been adopted as a baby. She was lucky to have been adopted by a loving family. Since she had a happy childhood, she'd only given her birth parents an occasional thought when she was a child. In college, though, she took a genetics class which piqued her interest in her biological background.

"Mike, I know how you feel. You know I was adopted too," she said. "If you have any questions or you want to talk about it, I'm here for you."

"Thanks, Mom. I'm okay."

Chapter 2 – Clearing His Head

Mike put on his running shoes and headed for the front door. He shouted to his mom that he was going out for a run. He often ran with his dad in the evenings, when it was much cooler. Even in October, it could get extremely hot in Florida. Mike felt the sweat start to bead on his forehead.

He and his dad usually ran by Robbie's house, and Robbie would sometimes join them. Today, Mike went in a different direction. His dad said running was a good way to clear his head. And today, Mike wanted to clear his head.

He liked the sound of his shoes pounding the asphalt: *ka-thump, ka-thump, ka-thump*. He felt the nice rhythm to it. Because he had long legs, it didn't take him long to go a few blocks.

After running the length of his street, he turned to

go into the next neighborhood. Many of the houses displayed colorful Halloween decorations. Pumpkins, scarecrows, ghosts, tombstones, and even a few deflated balloon characters lay wilted on the grass. They'd come alive at sunset. *Those must be houses with kids,* he thought.

He enjoyed Halloween. He had good memories of trick-or-treating with his older brother and sister. Now that he thought about it, he had many great memories with his family. The holidays were the best.

He picked up his pace. He wanted to run far, far away. Maybe he'd keep running and never come back. Everything was different now. He felt different.

Chapter 3 – Losing His Best Friend

Robbie was in his bedroom, throwing a tennis ball against the wall. He was in a bad mood and hoped his older brother would not pick today to be obnoxious. Robbie and Henry shared a room, and Henry liked to boss him around—sometimes, for no reason.

"Hey, squirt," Henry said, stepping into the room a few moments later. "What's up? I thought you were at Mike's house." Henry sat on his bed.

Robbie didn't answer. He scowled and continued bouncing the ball.

"Hey, you! I'm talking to you," Henry said.

"Leave me alone," Robbie said. "I didn't feel like playing anymore."

"Aw, did he whip your behind in a video game?"

"No, he did not. I was winning, if you must know." He threw the ball at his brother, hitting him on the forehead.

"Whoa there, tiger. Do you really want to start something with me? You still have bruises from the last time I had to teach you a lesson."

Robbie knew it was a mistake to challenge him. Henry had a bad temper, and when he lost it … well, it was not pretty. Both Henry and their dad had "anger control issues," as his mother put it. Robbie knew from experience that it was better to be invisible, stay quiet, and disappear when things got tense.

"Sorry 'bout that," Robbie said. "I'm just bored."

"Yeah, and you look pathetic … like you lost your best friend," Henry said. He flipped the ball back to Robbie and left the room.

Maybe I did, Robbie thought.

Chapter 4 – Family Time

About a mile away, Manuel Martinez helped his grandmother pick some carrots from her backyard vegetable garden. He hated eating carrots, but didn't mind picking them. He enjoyed spending time with his *abuela.*

Manuel's grandparents, who had come from Mexico many years ago, lived with his family. The small house sometimes got a little crowded; still, no one seemed to mind. It had always been that way, so having three generations under one roof seemed normal to Manuel.

Maria, Manuel's sister, often helped Manuel with his homework. He wasn't a big fan of reading and he hated math. Manuel preferred being outside and thought school was a huge waste of time. Someday he hoped to own a farm or maybe a grove. He knew he would have to learn more about agriculture and figured he could get that from work experience.

He thought, *What does math have to do with growing things, anyway?*

Maria, on the other hand, loved school. She was a sophomore in high school and already planned to go to college. Maria worked hard to get good grades. She participated in many extracurricular activities; they could help her get a scholarship. No one in the Martinez family had gone to college, and she intended to be the first.

"Dinner's almost ready," their mother announced from the kitchen. "Manuel, wash up, and Maria, please set the table."

Manuel was hoping his mother had made his favorite dish, chicken enchiladas. She was a good cook and she always put plenty of food on the table. His grandmother's fresh herbs made everything even tastier. Dinner at the Martinez house was always a time for sharing the day's events, often with some good-natured teasing. Meals were often noisy, but provided valuable family time together.

Chapter 5 – Who Are We?

Because it was raining on Monday, Mike's dad gave Mike a ride to school on his way to work. Mike often walked with Robbie; however, the two hadn't spoken since their Saturday spat. Robbie arrived at the same time that Mike was getting out of the car.

"Hey," Robbie said, looking embarrassed.

"Hey," Mike said, with a shrug of his shoulder. He turned his gaze aside quickly.

They walked in silence toward their fifth-grade classroom.

After several long, awkward moments, Robbie said, "Look, I'm sorry for being a jerk. I didn't mean to spout off like that. Sometimes I say the wrong thing."

"It's okay," Mike said. "I know I'm adopted, so it's no big deal."

"Still friends?" Robbie asked.

"Sure."

When they entered their classroom, Ms. Johansson was writing some strange words on the whiteboard. After she finished, she stood back and smiled. By then, everyone was at their assigned desk.

She scanned the room and said, "Students, as you know, we've been discussing the early colonization of America. We will be studying the American Revolution, how our country became a nation, and how its principles, as stated in the Declaration of Independence, are still important today. Now I want to add another dimension to who we are as a country." She paused and looked at her students. "Who are we?"

No one answered. Several students had puzzled expressions on their faces. Others had blank stares.

"What do you mean, Ms. Johansson?" said Fiona, a redheaded girl in the front row.

"I mean, who are the people who make up the United States? Where did they come from? And why is that significant today?"

Again, total silence from the class.

Finally, Annie, a Black girl in the back of the room said, "My family comes from Ohio. Is that what you mean?"

"Yes," said Ms. Johansson. "That's exactly what I mean. You and your parents came to Florida from Ohio. Taking it one step further, where did their parents and your great-grandparents come from?"

Ms. Johansson held up a hand and said, "Annie, that's really a question for another time. For now, we know we all have roots that go back to other places. Our country is often referred to as a melting pot because our population is a mixture of so many different ethnic groups and cultures. I want us to understand who we are as a country, not only by studying events and people from the past, but by discovering who we are as people."

She gestured to the front of the room. "Those words I've written on the board may look foreign to you today. I hope they will look familiar in a few weeks."

Chapter 6 – Some of Us Are Different

During lunch, Mike and Robbie sat in their usual spot in the cafeteria. Manuel asked if he could join them. Mike agreed. Robbie was not so friendly.

"What do you guys think about what Ms. Johansson was talking about earlier?" Manuel asked.

"Who knows?" Robbie said through a mouthful of a peanut-butter sandwich.

Manuel said, "I wish we could do something fun, like plant a garden, like we did in third grade, or do science experiments. I got a feeling this studying about people will require a lot of reading. I'd rather do something where we *actually do* something."

"Yeah," Robbie said. "I can't get excited about long-lost relatives. They're all dead, so what does that have to do with me?"

Mike remained quiet. He was thinking about his

family—except that he didn't know anything about his biological family, so this presented a problem.

When they finished their lunch, the students were allowed to go out on the playground until the bell rang.

Outside, Robbie and Mike stood apart from the others. Robbie asked, "Mike, why did you let that Mexican kid sit at our table? He's different from us and he makes bad grades. I don't want his stupidity to rub off on us."

"Robbie, you're crazy. I like him! You need to lighten up."

The two friends wandered over to a huge oak tree to get out of the sun. A group of girls was sitting under the tree, discussing their weekend plans. Another girl with long black hair was standing by herself, reading a book. She was in their class, but no one seemed to pay attention to her because she had an accent and was embarrassed when she had to talk or answer a question for Ms. Johansson.

Robbie asked, "Where do you suppose her family comes from?"

"I don't know," Mike said.

Her clothes were different from the other girls' and her name was hard to pronounce, so no one talked to her. She never smiled and always looked like she would rather be somewhere else.

The bell rang. The students walked slowly back into the building. The girl with the funny name stumbled and dropped her book. Manuel ran over, picked it up, and handed it to her.

"*Chokran*," she said in Lebanese.

"Huh?" Manuel said.

"I mean, thank you," she replied, a little embarrassed.

"*De nada*," Manuel said.

Chapter 7 – Where Did I Come From?

Mike found his mother in the utility room, putting clothes in the washer.

"Mom," Mike said, "you said I could talk to you about being adopted."

"Sure, what do you want to know?"

She pushed a button and closed the cover of the machine. He followed her to the dining room table, where they sat across from each other.

Mike told her about the discussion at school that day, that they were going to learn about their family histories. He told her he was concerned because he didn't know about his biological family. "I know I'm Black, like you and Dad," Mike said, "but that's all I know."

"We've never had this conversation before. I think you're ready for it now," she said. "We adopted you when you were six months old. We knew we wanted another child, and that's when you came along. A lawyer friend of ours called to tell us about a baby boy who needed a good home."

She let that sink in, and then continued by telling Mike that his parents had died in a terrible car wreck. He had been left in the care of his grandmother, who was not in good health. His grandmother had been diagnosed with cancer and was undergoing treatments that left her unable to care for a baby.

"Your father and I fell in love with you the minute we saw you," she said, with tears in her eyes. "That was one of the happiest days of my life. And your brother and sister were as excited as we were to make you a part of our family."

Mike thought about it for a while, and then asked if they knew any details about his birth parents.

"Your mother was a teacher and your father was a police officer. We have some documents we can share with you that tell more about them. I'll get them out tonight, and we can go over them with your dad. Your birth certificate lists your name as Michael, but we've always called you Mike. We'll be glad to answer any questions you have," she said. "And Mike, we can do research online that should be able to tell us more. I worked with a genealogist to learn more about my heritage. We can do that for you too, if you'd like."

It was a lot for Mike to process. He was eager to learn more about his biological family, but also a little nervous. What would he find?

Chapter 8 – Family History

At school the next day, Ms. Johansson announced that a special guest would be visiting their class after lunch.

"I hope it's not the police officer who speaks to us every year about not talking to strangers. We're too old for that stuff," Robbie said quietly.

Manuel said, "I hope this person speaks for a long, long time, so we won't have to do math."

Unfortunately for Manuel, Ms. Johansson moved their math lesson to the morning. After lunch, when the students returned to their classroom, their teacher introduced them to a tall woman with long blond hair.

"Class, this is Mrs. Tucker. She is a genealogist, and she's here to tell you how she helps people trace their family histories. Let's welcome her with a big round of applause."

After the clapping stopped, Mrs. Tucker stepped away from Ms. Johansson and looked at the students. She said, "Who likes history?"

Johnny, a boy who rarely talked, raised his hand immediately. Robbie and Mike looked at each other and then back at Johnny. They wondered why he would like history.

Mrs. Tucker clarified the reason for her question. "Genealogy is your family's history. Using documents that are from reliable sources, we can determine who our ancestors are, where they came from, and even what they did. Genealogy gives us our own personal history."

"This is gonna be worse than math," Manuel said under his breath. He sighed and slid down in his chair.

Mrs. Tucker surveyed the room and asked for a show of hands. "Does anyone have grandparents who tell old family stories? Has anyone heard stories about a family member, maybe a great-grandfather, who may have been a soldier?"

A hand shot up. It belonged to Margaret, who was talkative. Seeing Margaret on the edge of her chair,

Robbie chuckled and rolled his eyes.

Mrs. Tucker nodded to Margaret, and said, "Or maybe someone who marched with Martin Luther King for equality, in the 1960s? You can find these answers through historical records."

Mrs. Tucker called on Johnny, who had his hand up.

He said, "My mom told me her great-grandfather was an Indian cowboy."

Robbie laughed out loud. "No, he wasn't," Robbie mumbled.

"Seriously, he was," Johnny said, turning at his desk to face Robbie. "He was a Seminole cowboy."

Robbie laughed again. "That's an oxymoron! You know, a contradiction … Indians and cowboys. Hello?"

"Actually, Johnny is accurate," Mrs. Tucker said. "There were Indian cowboys here in Florida. Their history, which is mostly oral, has proven to be significant to Florida's beginnings. Oral history, which is spoken out loud, is often recorded on tapes or videos or other audio devices. If it isn't, one day that history could disappear."

Margaret raised her hand again. "I think my great-grandfather was a pilot in World War II. I've heard some stories from my grandpa," she said. "One day, I'd like to be a pilot too."

Robbie chuckled again and shook his head from side to side. Margaret frowned at him.

Mrs. Tucker smiled and gave a nod to Margaret's high-flying ambition, saying, "That's awesome!"

Using Margaret's comment as an example, Mrs. Tucker said, "There are military records giving us information, such as where your great-grandfather was located during World War II. You may even discover in what battles he flew," she added.

Margaret bubbled over with even more excitement, while Mike slid down in his seat, thinking, *I just wish I knew who my grandfather was.*

Mrs. Tucker said, "Every ten years, there is a census taken by our government. This census tells us where our ancestors lived, their occupation, and how old they were at the time of the census. And there are many different types of records kept here, locally, in your hometown. From the time you were born, recordings have been made of your existence."

This information got the students making comments to each other.

The genealogist waited for their attention to return to the front of the room. "But remember, we can only trace our ancestry where there are written documents that list information on people. Sometimes papers have been destroyed in fires, or in war, or in some cases, countries didn't keep detailed records. In fact, before slavery was abolished in our country, the records on many of the enslaved people did not contain important details like their names."

The room was quiet; she could see that the students were showing more interest.

She took a deep breath. "Using these records, along with documented historical events," Mrs. Tucker said, "you can recreate your ancestors' life paths. You only need the smallest amount of family information to begin to find these records." She took a few steps back and gave a nod to Ms. Johansson, at her desk.

"Class, Mrs. Tucker is going to teach us how to

trace our family histories," Ms. Johansson said. "To help us do that, I have an assignment for you that will get us started."

She handed out papers titled Family History Worksheet, and asked the students to interview their family members for details about each of them, such as their full name and when and where they were born. She also passed out copies of a letter for their parents, elaborating on the family history project. She told the class that if any parents had questions or concerns about this, they should contact her.

"I want your parents to understand that we will protect your family's privacy. You will be the one dealing with your family's information. And if they prefer that you not participate in this project, I will have another assignment for you that will support our study into our country's history without using any of your personal information."

Standing next to Mrs. Tucker, Ms. Johansson said, "We'll use the information you'll fill in on your Family History Worksheet to kick-start your online research for creating your family tree. These worksheets will be due on Monday, so you have the rest of the week to work on them. And thank you, Mrs. Tucker, from all of us."

Chapter 9 – Gathering Family Data

Walking home that afternoon, Robbie was especially quiet.

"What do you think about today's assignment?" Mike asked Robbie. "My parents already told me we're going to do some research about my birth family. This is kinda cool."

Robbie shrugged. "I think it's kinda dumb. Plus, my dad doesn't like to talk about his family. This won't be easy."

* * *

When Manuel got home that afternoon, he threw his backpack down on his bed and headed outside to the garden.

"How was school today?" his grandmother asked.

"It was okay. We had a lady who talked to us about family histories," he said. "It was kinda interesting, except then our teacher gave us an assignment to talk to our relatives to learn more about who we are."

His grandmother was silent while she pruned the lower stems on the tomato plants.

She paused her work and said, "You know that your grandfather and I came from Mexico. We still have relatives in Veracruz, and some of our ancestors were influential people. You should talk to your grandfather about it. He's very proud of his family."

"Nobody ever told me this," Manuel said.

He sat on the ground next to his grandmother, and began pulling weeds and thinking about what life must have been like in Mexico. He had never thought about that before.

* * *

Throughout the week, students were asking their parents, grandparents, aunts, and uncles for information about themselves and their ancestors. Johnny Griffin confirmed his great-grandfather was a Native American with Seminole roots. Fiona discovered she got her curly red hair from her Irish grandmother. Walter Diaz found out his grandfather almost drowned when the fishing boat he was on started to sink on its ninety-mile journey to Florida from Cuba in 1965.

Samuel Turner's father showed him photographs of relatives who had perished in the Holocaust. Samuel had heard about the Holocaust, but didn't know much about it. His father always became emotional when discussing it.

"The Holocaust was a terrible thing," his father said. "During World War II, the Nazis, under the leadership of Adolf Hitler, rounded up Jews throughout Europe and placed many of them in concentration camps. Estimates are that more than six million Jews were murdered."

Mr. Turner told Samuel it was critical that people remember it so it can never happen again. Samuel was shocked and saddened that such a horrible thing had happened to the Jews and that some of his relatives died because of it.

In other homes, phone calls were made to distant relatives. Some students had virtual visits, on their computers and cell phones, with cousins they had never met. Families retrieved documents and photographs from boxes and photo albums. Pieces of jewelry, military medals, old letters, and even musical instruments came out of attics and drawers. One student saw old movies of grandparents who had died before he was born.

Students were learning things they had never heard or seen before. And these stories were personal—not something they learned about in a book.

On Monday morning, most of the students couldn't wait to share with their classmates what they had discovered.

All but one.

Chapter 10 – Trick or Treat!

That weekend, Halloween was on Saturday. Manuel's parents insisted his sister go trick-or-treating with him. Maria didn't mind; she liked going out incognito. She wore an old prom dress she had found at a thrift store and added sparkly sandals. She topped off the attire with a bright pink wig, a tiara, and oversized purple sunglasses.

Manuel dressed up like a farmer. He borrowed his grandfather's straw hat that he had worn for years to keep the sun off his face while working in the orange groves. Large work gloves covered Manuel's hands, and he carried a gunnysack for collecting candy.

When the prom queen and the farmer walked past a local playground, they saw Robbie, his brother, and a couple other guys sitting on the hood of Henry's car, across the street in the parking lot. Henry and his friends were making fun of the costumes the trick-or-treaters wore.

"Let's walk faster," Manuel said to his sister. "That kid over there is in my class, and he likes to pick on me."

Maria recognized Henry from high school and knew he was a bully, so it didn't surprise her that Robbie was one too.

"Hey, Robbie," Henry said, loud enough for everyone to hear, "do you know that kid over there?" He pointed at the sidewalk.

Robbie didn't answer. He looked away, embarrassed.

"Hey, Pinky, I like your pink hair. I have a special treat for you," Henry said, and threw a raw egg at Maria and Manuel. It missed them and splattered across the sidewalk.

Maria stared at the boys and then threw back her head and laughed. "Keep walking," she whispered to her brother. "Ignore them. They just want to get a reaction. Laughing at them is the best way to deal with them."

For the next hour, Manuel collected lots of candy. Sometimes he and Maria met up with his friends. About eight o'clock, Maria said it was time to go home. When they walked past the park again, they noticed more cracked eggs on the street and sidewalk. Fortunately, Henry and his friends, including Robbie, were in the far section of the park, playing basketball.

"They must have gotten tired of harassing people," Maria said. "Maybe it's time to give them a taste of their own medicine."

"What are you going to do?" Manuel asked nervously.

"Not sure. I'll think of something."

They hurried across the street. Maria told Manuel to keep a lookout. She peeked into Henry's car and saw an open egg carton with two eggs left in it. She quietly opened the car door and removed the eggs. She carefully placed one egg on the driver's seat and tucked it near the back, hoping it wouldn't be noticed before someone sat down. She put the other one over the visor on the driver's side. Then she and Manuel rushed back across the street.

"Don't you want to wait to see what happens?" Manuel said after she turned to go home.

"Oh, I know," Maria said. "He gave me a trick, so I'm giving him a treat! That's rather appropriate, don't you think?"

Chapter 11 – Making Connections

On Monday morning, the excitement in the classroom was noticeable. Students were sharing stories about their families. Ms. Johansson was beaming.

"I'm so glad you're excited about your assignment," she said."However, we've got to keep up with our regular studies, which we will do each morning. We can spend some afternoon time on our family histories and use the skills we're learning in math, science, social studies, and language arts to help with this research project."

Several students groaned aloud.

Nevertheless, the morning passed quickly. After lunch, Ms. Johansson tacked a large world map to the bulletin board. She asked each student to come up, one at a time, throughout the next few weeks and place red pins on the map to identify locations where their relatives had once lived.

"We're going to see the many different places where we have connections," she said. "I'm putting a world atlas next to the bulletin board. The atlas has bigger maps of the different countries, to help you find exact locations."

That afternoon she had each of them download onto their tablet, a template for a timeline. They would start adding data from their Family History Worksheet, specifically, the birth dates of relatives and historic events that affected their families.

Margaret asked, "You mean, like World War II?"

"Yes, and other significant historical events that your ancestors may have lived through."

Next, their teacher did a review of their recent social studies lesson on primary and secondary sources. She reminded the students that primary sources provided firsthand information. That would be from someone who had personally witnessed or participated in an event. Secondary sources were considered secondhand knowledge, which meant someone could add their own opinion or interpretation of something that had happened, or it was something someone else had told them.

"I want you to identify on your worksheets what kinds of sources you have," she said. "If one of your parents told you about things that happened to them, that would be a primary source. If a relative describes something they learned from another family member, then that would be a secondary source."

Robbie raised his hand. "Are we gonna get a grade on this?"

"Yes, you are," Ms. Johansson replied. "We'll be applying many of the things we've been studying in other subjects. Instead of answering questions from a textbook, we'll be using information that is real and personal to you. It's a fun way to learn these skills."

Robbie slumped in his chair and mumbled something under his breath.

Chapter 12 – Who's the Fastest?

Out on the playground after lunch, several of the boys were running races, trying to see who was the fastest. Mike said he liked to go distances, so he wasn't concerned about being fast. Robbie bragged that he could beat anyone in their class. Johnny accepted Robbie's challenge, and soon they were racing across the yard. Johnny finished two strides ahead of Robbie.

Jokingly, Johnny said, "Maybe I get my speed from my Seminole great-grandfather."

"You were just lucky," Robbie said, and took a step toward Johnny and looked like he was going to push him.

Witnessing this, two teachers intervened. One of them told Robbie to apologize to Johnny and to stand next to them until the lunch break was over.

Robbie stepped over to Johnny and loudly said he

was sorry so the teachers could hear.

Back in the classroom, though, Robbie told Johnny he'd see him after school and they'd settle this when no teachers were around.

Mike overheard Robbie's threat, and asked Johnny, "What are you gonna do?"

"Nothing," Johnny said. "Robbie's a bully. I plan to ignore him."

At the sound of the final bell, Robbie made a dash for the classroom door. Johnny was relieved; he didn't want to get into a fight with him.

When Johnny was walking home, Robbie suddenly jumped out from behind a parked car. He grabbed Johnny's backpack and threw it on the ground.

"Let's finish this," Robbie said, putting his fists in the air.

"There's nothing to finish," Johnny said. "We ran a race and I won."

"Winning a footrace is nothing. How are you with your fists?"

By now, other students had noticed the confrontation

and gathered around them.

Johnny said, "I don't want to fight with you."

"Yeah, you're scared you'll lose," Robbie said. He poked Johnny in the chest. "You think you're so smart because you claim you have Indian blood. I bet that's a bunch of baloney. Your grandfather probably made it up."

"Why would he make it up?" Johnny asked. "Don't you believe what your grandfather tells you?"

Robbie didn't know what to say. He hadn't talked to his grandfather in several years. He looked around and realized everyone was staring at him.

"It's nobody's business what my grandfather says. This whole family history project is dumb, and all of you are stupid for doing it!"

He noticed one of the parents coming in their direction. He kicked dirt on Johnny's backpack and quickly walked away.

Chapter 13 – Pieces to a Puzzle

The next day Mrs. Tucker revisited the class. This time she brought several documents with her to show on the overhead projector. The first one was her own birth certificate.

"Everyone has a birth certificate," she stated.

Robbie whispered to Mike, "This is gonna be boring."

"On this one document, we can find a great deal of information. Let's begin with the date and time of my birth," she said as she pointed to where that was listed.

"What else do you see?" she asked.

Emma raised her hand. Mrs. Tucker called on her.

"The names of your parents," Emma said.

"That's right," Mrs. Tucker responded. "What else do you see?"

Emma's hand went up again. After a nod from Mrs. Tucker, Emma answered, "The name of the hospital."

"Yes, the name and address of the hospital, including the city and state where a person was born. It gives the address of the parents, where they lived at the time of the birth," she said. "And look, next to their address, it gives us one more helpful piece of information—the state where the person's parents were born."

Mrs. Tucker paused, looking around the room to see if the students understood why she was pointing out this specific information.

"Every document tells a portion of the story of someone's life," she said. "So, I want you to think of each piece of information like a piece of a big puzzle. We are going to assemble a puzzle about your ancestors."

Robbie muttered to Mike, "Puzzles are fun. This is not."

"And there will be many, many pieces," Mrs. Tucker added.

Robbie groaned.

Mrs. Tucker introduced the students to a genealogy website where they could record data about their family members. Each student would start with themselves, adding their complete name and date of birth. Then they could add their parents' information, building their family trees. She noted there would be a box they could check for someone who was still alive and that would indicate that it was private information.

The students were eager to add names to their family trees on their tablets. Even Ms. Johansson was creating one with her Scandinavian family roots.

Mike had already started one. His mother had been helping him do some research at home. He had discovered that his father's family came from Virginia.

The students filled in their family trees with the data they had collected on their worksheets. Then Mrs. Tucker gave another demonstration, on how they could find military information online, providing them a website to check out.

"It's very simple," she stated. "Begin by filling in your ancestor's name and the state where he or she came from. Whether it's World War I, World War II, or even the Revolutionary War, there are records to show us where your ancestor may have served."

Robbie perked up and straightened up in his chair when he heard Mrs. Tucker mention military records.

Mike noticed and gave a little chuckle. *Maybe,* he thought, *Robbie will find a piece to his family's puzzle.*

Chapter 14 – Digging Deeper

While the students continued to explore the websites, Mrs. Tucker circulated around the room, answering questions and helping them navigate their way through the various documents.

"Mrs. Tucker, look what I found!" Fiona exclaimed. "My search revealed so many records. There are census records, birth records, and immigration records. My family must have lived in Boston in the late 1800s." Fiona was excitedly waving several pieces of paper she had printed off.

"When you're reviewing these websites," Mrs. Tucker said, "remember to look carefully at each document to be certain the reference is really for your ancestor."

As Mrs. Tucker approached Johnny, he asked, "Are there records on the Seminole Indians?"

Mrs. Tucker said yes and then announced to the

class, "Johnny has asked a good question that the entire class should hear. Go ahead, Johnny, ask your question again."

"Are there records on the Seminole Indians?"

"There are," she said. "There is something called the Dawes Rolls. It's a type of census of the Native American nations. The Dawes Rolls were a commissioned listing of those people living throughout the eastern Native American nations in the late 1800s. In the Dawes Rolls, you will find listings of the Creeks, Choctaw, Chickasaws, Cherokee, and Seminole nations' early members."

Mrs. Tucker shifted her gaze from the class, back to Johnny. "Don't get upset if you don't find what you're looking for there," she told him. "Think about this. On the day the Dawes Rolls were registering people, your ancestor could have been out on a hunt or moving cattle. We know some of those who are not listed in the Dawes Rolls are listed in other resources. For instance, *Seminole Roots, Volumes I and II* is another excellent source."

Throughout the afternoon the classroom exploded with squeals and excitement when students discovered names, documents, and photographs about their relatives.

Before the bell rang, Mrs. Tucker handed out papers and said, "Here's the reason I wanted you to hear Johnny's question earlier. We should know where to find different types of information. What I'm giving you is a sort of cheat sheet. Shhh … we won't tell anyone."

She held up the documents and explained. "This includes several websites you can visit, like the ones we learned about today, along with a few more. On the second sheet, a list of dates will coincide with military events in our history. When we come back next week, I would like each of you to have searched some of these sites and report back to me any connections you've discovered."

Robbie sat at his desk with his arms folded over his chest and an angry look on his face.

From the front of the room, Ms. Johansson noticed, and asked, "Robbie, where is your Family Tree Worksheet?"

"I lost it," he replied.

"Do you need another one?"

He said, "I couldn't do it because information about my family is nobody's business, and it's a stupid project."

Several of the other students exchanged wide-eyed looks. Ms. Johansson asked Robbie to step up to her desk. She quietly said she didn't want anyone to be offended by this research project. She would give him another assignment to work on today. She added that she would call his parents to give them details of the project so they would not be offended.

Robbie asked her not to call his house. He said he'd get in trouble. Ms. Johansson said she needed to do it so there would be no misunderstandings. No one was trying to invade their privacy, and if they preferred that Robbie not participate in their project, she would respect that.

"Ms. Johansson," he begged, "if you have to call my house, please talk only to my mother."

She promised she would, and from her desk drawer she pulled out another assignment for him. The rest of the day, he'd research the early immigrants who came to America.

"You can start by learning about Ellis Island."

Chapter 15 – It's Time You Know

When Robbie got home that afternoon, he went straight to his bedroom and slammed the door. A few minutes later, his mother knocked on his door.

"Robbie," she called, "may I come in?"

Sitting at his desk, he groaned, and then said okay.

His mother sat on the edge of his bed. She said she had gotten a call from his teacher, who told her about the family research project.

"Why didn't you tell us about it?" she said. "It sounds interesting."

"Mom, you know how Dad is. He doesn't wanna talk about his family. I didn't wanna make him mad."

Mrs. Langford sighed. "Let me tell you a story," she said. "Your father and I got married when we were very young. My parents didn't want me to marry him, but I was—I mean, we were in love. Your father was embarrassed because his family didn't have a lot of money. His father worked in the orange groves, and his mother was a cashier in a grocery store. Neither of his parents had graduated from high school, and that bothered him."

Robbie said, "Is that why we never go visit his parents anymore?"

"Yes, that's part of the reason. I think your father is ashamed of the way he acted toward his parents, so he avoided seeing them. After his mother died, we visited them much less."

"That's sad," Robbie said. "I always liked Grandpa Langford. And I remember Grandma. She was always baking something."

"I'm glad to hear that," his mom said. "Those memories are special. Your great-grandparents were some of the earliest residents of this area, before this part of Florida became popular with tourists. They faced lots of hardships, but they persevered. It's people like that who built this community and even this country. We should be proud of them."

Robbie thought about that. *Isn't that why Ms. Johansson wanted us to do this project?*

"Robbie, if you want to learn more about our family and our ancestors, I can give you their names and other information about many of them."

"What if Dad finds out and doesn't like it?"

"I'll deal with him," she said. "It's time you know where you come from and who you are."

Chapter 16 – A Melting Pot

On Monday when their worksheets were due, Ms. Johansson asked the students to share the discoveries about their relatives. Many hands shot into the air, some waving around; the students were eager to tell some stories.

Johnny said he had done research on the internet about the Seminole Indians. He discovered that the Seminole Tribe was a lot like the rest of the United States—a melting pot. It was made up of several Native American tribes and many Africans seeking freedom.

"So," Johnny said, "I asked my grandfather about the Seminoles. Instead of telling me about our history, he said he'd show me."

"How'd he do that?" Margaret asked.

"He took me to St. Augustine, where we went to a place called Fort Mose. It's spelled M-o-s-e, and it's pronounced Moh-say. It was the first free Black community in the United States. Many enslaved Black people ran away from plantations in the Carolinas and Georgia." Johnny picked up his research paper. "They were granted asylum there by the king of Spain, who had claimed that part of Florida. I looked up 'asylum' and it means 'shelter from danger or hardship.' That's all I have for now," Johnny said, putting his notes down on his desk.

Ms. Johansson told the class that Fort Mose was the first legally sanctioned, or formally approved, free Black community because Africans seeking asylum there agreed to be baptized into the Catholic Church. She added that Fort Mose also became part of the original Underground Railroad.

"What was that?" Mike asked.

She said the Underground Railroad later grew into a secret network that helped enslaved people escape to free states in the north, in the years before the Civil War.

"People sympathetic to those seeking a better life provided special routes and safe places to hide," she said.

"Most of the people using the Underground Railroad went north, but some traveled south to Florida, and many of them got help from the Native Americans."

"And that's how I'm connected to Fort Mose," Johnny said, feeling proud. "My grandpa said that when he was a boy, his grandfather told him that his people had worked on a plantation in Georgia and left it to find a better life in Florida. They eventually connected with some Native Americans, who later became known as the Seminoles."

Ms. Johansson asked Johnny how he felt after visiting a place where his ancestors might have spent time.

Johnny thought for several long moments. The classroom became quiet when the students noticed how serious Johnny had become.

"It made it all real," he answered. "I understood the history better after I visited that place. And now I want to learn more about what it was like for the people who were there."

Ms. Johansson gave Johnny a thumbs-up.

Annie asked, "What did you see at the fort?"

He looked at his notepaper. "It's officially called Fort Mose Historic State Park and it has a boardwalk on the water. The visitor center has lots of cool stuff. It shows how the people lived and tells some of their stories," Johnny said. "Oh! I even learned that one of them, Francisco Menendez, fought in an Indian War in South Carolina, and then escaped to Florida with some Indian friends, and later became a corsair—that's a pirate!"

Robbie laughed. "First you tell us Indians were cowboys, and now you say one of the enslaved men who came to Fort Mose was a pirate. That's crazy!"

"It's all true. Look it up if you don't believe me," Johnny said. "I don't see you sharing any stories about your ancestors."

Robbie had no answer for that.

Chapter 17 – Life Isn't Always Fair

Ms. Johansson asked if any other students had exciting stories to share.

Fiona said her mother had retrieved some photo albums from the attic. They were pictures of her great-grandparents. She held up an old black-and-white photograph of a man and a woman with serious expressions on their faces. They were standing in front of a house with a thatched roof.

"This was taken in Ireland. My mom says back then they didn't smile when their pictures were taken," Fiona said. "She also told me many Irish people came to America during a potato famine. People in Ireland were starving. That would make them sad!"

Samuel raised his hand excitedly. "Ms. Johansson, I saw a photo of some of my relatives in Poland, and they look serious, like Fiona's. Of course, they had a good reason not to smile."

"Samuel, why don't you tell the class what you're referring to?" Ms. Johansson said.

Samuel, who was known as the class clown, had a somber look on his face. He said he found out that several of his Polish relatives, those who didn't emigrate to America, disappeared during World War II.

"What happened to them?" Manuel asked.

"They were rounded up by the Nazis and sent to concentration camps. They were never heard from again," he said sadly.

Ms. Johansson said, "The Holocaust was a terrible chapter in world history. It's sad to know how inhumane human beings can be. Unfortunately, it happened. You will study it later in school, but it's essential that we remember the bad things that occurred so they will never happen again."

"Yeah, like the Trail of Tears," Johnny added. "My dad told me about that terrible event—and it happened right here in America."

Ms. Johansson took a deep breath and said, "The Trail

of Tears was when the United States government made thousands of Native Americans leave the lands where their families had lived for many years, and forced them to move west of the Mississippi River. Many of them had to walk and, of course, many of them died along the way."

Mike asked, "Why did our government do that?"

"Many of the settlers wanted the Indians removed so they could have the land," Johnny said with disgust.

"That doesn't seem fair," Samuel said.

"It certainly wasn't fair," Ms. Johansson said. "And that's what history teaches us. Some of you are finding that you have direct connections to events from the past."

Walter shared that his grandfather left Cuba after a revolution there. With six friends, he came to the United States as a refugee, in a fishing boat. He had to leave his parents behind. They would not leave their home. He had no money and spoke very little English.

"My dad gets sad when he talks about this," Walter said.

Ms. Johansson could see that some of these stories

were upsetting the students.

"I think you'll find that many of these stories have happy endings. All of you are proof of that," she said. "Now that you have an idea of what countries your relatives came from, let's research the customs, foods, and ways they made a living. You might find that we have much in common with each other, even though we come from different backgrounds."

Chapter 18 – Mike's Journey Begins

When Mike got home that afternoon, his mother was in the kitchen fixing lasagna, his favorite meal. She told him that a guest was coming for dinner.

"Your biological father's cousin is in town, and I invited him to join us."

Mike got a panicked look on his face. "Mom, I'm not sure I'm ready for this," he said.

"You have nothing to feel awkward about. You should be excited."

"I am, but—"

Just then, the doorbell chimed. His mother patted him on the head and went to answer the door. Mike could hear a man's deep voice … apologizing for coming early.

"No problem," Mike's mother said. "Come on in and have a seat. I'll get Mike. He just got home from school.

This will give you two some time to visit before we eat."

When she came back into the kitchen, Mike was sitting at the kitchen table, slumped over. She smiled at him, kissed him on the forehead, and escorted him into the living room.

He saw a tall Black man looking at Mike's childhood photos scattered on the coffee table. He was holding one that showed Mike in a baseball uniform. The man stood up when he saw Mike.

"Hello there, Mike. I'm your cousin Edward Goins, but you can call me Eddie. I've been very eager to meet you," he said.

Mike stared at him for a moment. In a subdued voice, Mike said, "Hi."

"I'm enjoying looking at these pictures of you. I have a son a little older than you and he plays baseball too," he said. "Your father was a good baseball player. In fact, he was a good athlete. His favorite sport was track. He used to run marathons."

Mike's eyes lit up. "I like to run, too. Maybe I got that from him."

Eddie smiled, crossed his arms across his chest, and shook his head back and forth. "You look like a smaller version of your father. I want to learn all about you, and I'll tell you anything you want to know about your parents and the rest of our family."

Mike's journey into his heritage had already begun.

Chapter 19 – Exciting Discoveries

After Eddie left, Mike's mom logged on to her computer and opened the files that Eddie had emailed her. She discovered his family had done extensive research into the family genealogy.

When reading the detailed chart, she followed the generations back, one after another. An hour later, she realized Mike descended from one of the earliest documented Africans to arrive in Virginia.

"Wow!" she exclaimed. "In 1619. That's even before the *Mayflower* arrived!" She couldn't believe her eyes. "Mike, come and look at this."

Mike could tell his mom was really excited. She gestured for him to sit beside her.

"Look," his mom said. She pointed out the date on the computer screen. "Mike, you have some deep roots in our country's history. This is incredible!"

They continued to sit in awe as they processed each word. Mike's ancestors had lived through several challenging events, and it seemed they only found themselves in Virginia by accident.

Mike's mom read aloud: "The Africans aboard a cargo ship traveling from Africa to New Spain were stolen by two English pirates."

"New Spain? Where is that?" Mike asked.

"Today it's called Mexico. Back in 1619, the people were under Spanish rule, so it wasn't known as Mexico yet."

In the next few minutes, Mike and his mom uncovered one amazing event after another. With each new realization, Mike sat up straighter.

"Times must have been awful rough back then," Mike's mother said. "It says here, the Africans helped save the Virginia settlers from starvation after the Native American uprising of 1622. The Africans knew how to grow crops and raise livestock. They were able to grow and replenish the food to feed everyone."

Mike felt exhilarated. He was related to people who helped start this country!

Chapter 20 – Coming to America

Meanwhile, at the kitchen table, David was looking at some Japanese immigration papers that his father had given him to examine. He could only read the documents that were in English. The items from Japan had writing that looked more like artwork instead of letters. He decided to ask his dad to translate them for him when he got home from work.

It would be fun to learn how to read and write in Japanese, David thought.

* * *

At Emma's house, her mother told her that her grandfather, Emma's great-grandfather, had come to America from Finland when he was twenty-one years old. She said he had entered the country through Ellis Island in New York.

Emma went to the website Mrs. Tucker had given

them and was able to find her great-grandfather listed on a New York ship manifest for a ship arriving in 1911. The document gave the ship's name, his age, nationality, last place of residence, and his original name.

Wanting to learn more about Ellis Island, Emma checked out additional websites. She found that many immigrants changed their names when they came to the United States. Some of their last names were difficult to spell and pronounce, and some people wanted to make their names sound more American. Emma's great-grandfather's Finnish first name was Heikki; however, he was later listed as Henry on his marriage license in 1916 and on the 1920 census records.

She learned that approximately 40 percent of Americans today descend from an immigrant who passed through Ellis Island. When Emma's great-grandfather went through the immigration process, no visas or passports were required, like they are today. However, they did have to pass a medical examination and legal inspection.

Emma's mother told her that her great-grandfather

took a freight train to Oregon, where his older sister lived. As many immigrants did, one family member would come to America first and then send for others, to help them get settled in their new country.

"Mom, did he speak English?" she asked.

"No, he didn't. He settled in a place where there were many others from Finland who had come to America, so he had other people who spoke the same language," her mother said. "And he came with very little money, which was the case for many immigrants."

She went on to tell Emma that many immigrants settled in places where others from their home country went before them—for example, German people in Pennsylvania, French people in Louisiana, Scandinavian people in the Midwest, and Polish people in the Great Lakes area of their new country.

"They were looking for a better life. Some wanted to escape political oppression, religious persecution, war, and famine. Many of them took difficult jobs after they got here so they could earn a living. They helped build America into what it is today," she said with pride in her voice.

"I can't wait to share this with my classmates," Emma said. "I wonder if they'll have similar stories."

Chapter 21 – See It for Myself

Margaret could hardly wait until her father got home from work. She wanted to know more about her great-great-grandfather. Her mother had told her she thought he was part of the Tuskegee Airmen, a famous group of Black aviators during World War II.

Soon after her father got home, he went up to the attic and brought down a box full of photographs, documents, and medals.

"There are some letters in here that my grandfather wrote to my grandmother while he was stationed in Italy during the war," Margaret's father said. "You might find them interesting. He couldn't tell her where he was exactly, for security reasons, so he talked about what it was like to be in Italy."

Spellbound by what she heard, Margaret sat near her dad on the living room sofa. Her mother, also interested, had taken a seat next to her daughter.

"You have to remember," her father said. "Most of the soldiers had never been to a foreign country before, so not only were they a long way from home, they were in a strange new place."

"And they were fighting in a war," Margaret added, her voice sad. "I never thought about that before. But then, I've never really thought about what happens to soldiers in a war."

She was quiet for a long time. Her parents left her alone with her thoughts. She sifted through the photographs and read a few of the letters.

This is much better than reading a history book, she thought. *I want to learn more.*

Back at her computer, she did some research on women who were famous pilots and astronauts. She learned about Amelia Earhart, the first female to fly solo across the Atlantic Ocean. And Bessie Coleman, who was the first woman of African American and Native American descent to hold a pilot's license. Margaret found women who pioneered in aviation came from

India, Russia, Thailand, Turkey, France, Sweden, and, of course, the United States.

She had heard about the US female astronauts, Christa McAuliffe and Sally Ride. Margaret had no idea there were so many others. She wanted to ask her parents if they could visit the Kennedy Space Center someday soon to learn more about the history and future of space travel.

I want to see that place for myself, she thought. *Like Johnny did.*

* * *

Yasmine was helping her mother prepare tabbouleh, a Lebanese salad dish. Her mother was also roasting a chicken for dinner.

"We'll have enough left over for you to take for your lunch tomorrow," her mother said.

"Mother, my lunches are not like what the other students bring," Yasmine said. "It makes me feel unusual. Why is our food so different from theirs?"

Her mother was glad to answer her daughter's question. "It is based on ingredients the people could find close to where they lived—the same as food in any culture. This is why Lebanese cooking uses lots of herbs, olive oil, garlic, and fresh meats such as chicken, fish, and lamb. I cook the way my mother cooked and her mother before her," she said. "And these are the foods that your father likes. That's what he ate when growing up."

Yasmine said she would like to have more American foods in their home. She especially wanted pizza.

"So, you want pizza?" her mother said. "You know our flatbread is similar to the pizza crust. We like tomatoes too, so maybe we can make a Lebanese pizza this weekend."

Yasmine laughed and said she'd like that.

Chapter 22 – Hey, You!

Maria Martinez was walking home from school when Henry Langford drove by in his beat-up old car, the one she had helped "treat" with raw eggs.

This could be trouble, she thought, when the car made a turn into the street that she'd have to cross. She was wondering if he remembered her from the Halloween escapade.

"Hey, you," he said. "Aren't you in my English class?"

"Are you talking to me?" she said with a disdainful look on her face.

"Yeah, you. I think we're in the same English class."

Evidently, Henry didn't remember her from that night.

"I have a name. It's Maria, not *hey you.*"

"Okay, Ma-ri-a," he said, pronouncing every syllable with emphasis. "Have you written the essay we gotta do for English class?"

Feeling awkward, she stopped before she reached the intersection. After all, she did trash his car, and maybe he had plans to get even. She decided she'd adopt a friendlier attitude, just in case.

"Yes, I've done my rough draft."

"Can I see it?" Henry asked.

"Why?"

"I thought I could get some ideas from it. I'm not so good at these things."

"No, I can't do that," she said. "First, it wouldn't be right. Second, you need to pick another book because my paper is on *Animal Farm,* so it would not work for you."

"Why would you pick a book about farm animals?" he asked.

"Have you read *Animal Farm*?" she said, trying to keep the sarcasm out of her voice.

"No. Why would I want to do that?"

She shook her head and looked away. She said, "I have to go home to finish my homework."

"I bet you're one of those who likes to get straight As. I don't get it," he said. "I'm happy with a C, even a D, as long as I pass. Why do you work so hard?"

"I'm trying to earn a scholarship so I can get a college education, and someday have a decent-paying job. Do you get that?"

He got out of the car and leaned against it. He glared at her. "You think I can't get a decent-paying job? My dad works in a manufacturing plant. He doesn't have a college degree, and I bet he makes more money than your dad. I could get a job there tomorrow if I wanted."

"Is that what you really want?" she said before she could stop herself.

He didn't answer. He stared at the ground a few seconds, nudged a pebble with his foot, and looked back up at her with sadness in his eyes. He returned to the driver's seat and, before he left, said, "*Adios!*" And drove off.

Chapter 23 – Discoveries in a Graveyard

On the playground the next day, Manuel asked Mike, "Wanna go with me to the old Beulah Cemetery after school tomorrow?"

"Why would you want to go there?" Mike said. "Graveyards freak me out!"

"My grandmother told me some of our relatives are buried there. I'd like to see it for myself, but I don't want to go alone."

Mike thought about it a few seconds. "Okay," he said. "We need to go right after school, though—before it gets dark."

The day after, when they were leaving school, Robbie joined them and asked where they were going. Manuel told him, and Robbie said they were crazy.

"Maybe we are. Maybe it's something I gotta do," Manuel said. "You can come with us if you want …

unless you're scared."

Robbie scoffed and said, "Nothing scares me. I'll go along to help protect you two. You never know what you might find."

They walked several blocks in silence, each lost in his thoughts. Approaching the wrought-iron fence that surrounded the graveyard, they slowed down in front of the entrance. A large black crow stared menacingly at them from one of the tombstones.

"Here goes nothing," Robbie said, and pushed the creaking gate open. "Should I find something to scare off the ghosts?"

"Cool it, Robbie," Mike said. "We're here to find Manuel's relatives. Why don't we split up so we can find them faster?"

Manuel told them the names would be Martinez and some could be Lopez. Some of them came to Florida in the 1930s, so their birth years could have been as early as the late 1800s.

Mike wandered over to several family plots; some were surrounded by a fence and others had large granite markers proclaiming the family name. Some had statues of angels and elaborate headstones etched with quotes from Scripture or famous poems. Many of them listed military service, and, by checking the dates Mike could figure out in which wars they had served.

Manuel discovered a section with many Hispanic names, and assumed they had their own section. Soon he found markers with names that looked familiar.

"Hey, Mike," he called, "I think I found some."

Mike hurried over, careful to step on the grassy areas between the graves. They stood, quietly reading several of the markers that listed the name, the birth year, and the year of death.

Manuel said, "I'm glad that my grandparents are still alive, but I think my great-grandmother is buried here somewhere. My mother's grandfather was killed in World War II and was buried in France."

"Let's find your great-grandmother," Mike said.

It took some searching before they located her grave. Manuel ran his fingers over her name. He pulled a paper out of his backpack and wrote down the dates listed on her headstone. He found a few other markers that could be family members. He made a list of their names to ask his grandparents about them when he got home. He noted the locations of the graves.

"Next time," he said, "I'm bringing a camera so I can take photos for my Family History folder."

"Let's go," Mike said. "It's getting dark. Where's Robbie?"

"He's probably hiding and waiting to jump out and scare us," Manuel said.

What they saw next shocked them both. Robbie was on the other side of the cemetery, on his knees, in front of a small headstone. He swiped an arm across his face and got up when he heard the boys coming.

The three of them stood there silently, not knowing what to say.

After a long pause, Robbie said, "I thought my grandmother might be buried here. I think this is her grave. I remember her. She made me feel special and was always baking cookies when we went to visit. My favorite was her oatmeal cookies with raisins. Every time I see oatmeal cookies, I think of her," he said.

After a long silence, Robbie told them, "I'm bringing flowers the next time I come."

Chapter 24 – Let's Do a Program!

"Ms. Johansson, what are we going to do with all this information we're collecting?" Fiona asked, the next day.

The class had their genealogy information ready at their desks.

"What would you like to do?" she replied.

The students offered several suggestions. One said they could do oral reports to share with their classmates what they'd found. Another student thought they should create displays, like they did with their science projects. Or they could form a club, another student suggested, and share their stories.

"Would you like to take this beyond our classroom and share it with your families?" their teacher asked. "You might know that we often invite our families to school for a turkey dinner on the day before Thanksgiving.

How about this year, we do a program for our families and show them what we've discovered?"

A loud resounding "Yes" echoed around the room. Students started proposing ideas.

"We could serve some of the foods we've learned about, instead of turkey," Samuel said. "We'll get plenty of that on Thanksgiving Day!"

One student thought they should create displays showing photographs and family items. Another one of the girls thought they could wear clothing that reflected their ethnic heritage.

"I wanna have music," Walter said. "There's always music at our family gatherings."

Ms. Johansson let them brainstorm more ideas while she listed them on the board. She said they'd have to work in small groups to get it done in time. They had only ten days until the Thanksgiving break.

Soon the classroom was buzzing like a beehive, with chairs and desks moved into small clusters, ideas shared, and frequent high-fives exchanged. Ms. Johansson circulated around the room, answering questions, making suggestions, and letting the students take ownership of the program.

Robbie had not joined any of the groups. He was looking at his tablet when Ms. Johansson asked him what interested him. He told her he didn't know where he fit in since he hadn't found anything unique about his family, like the others had.

"Why don't I help you dig a little deeper and see what we can find?"

They spent the next half hour searching family names in the genealogy records, based on the names and dates his mother had given him. They discovered a distant relative had already done extensive research on their family and listed the data on one of the websites. It showed that Robbie's grandfather was related to someone who had helped provide supplies to the colonial soldiers during the American Revolution.

Robbie beamed. The military records documented that his sixth great-grandfather was a farmer in Massachusetts who had provided food, horses, and equipment to the troops when the war broke out against

England in 1775.

"Even though he was only a farmer, he contributed too,"Robbie said, feeling happy for his ancestor's deeds. "I never knew this. I bet my dad doesn't know either. I can't wait to tell him!"

Chapter 25 – You Can't Make This Up!

At home that night, Mike and his mother resumed their research into his birth family's history. They began with a quick Google search focusing on keywords from the information Eddie had provided. They also found that the 400th anniversary of the first Africans to arrive in English America had been commemorated in 2019.

"Even though we missed it, we can still be proud of our 400-year history," his mom said.

They continued to look, and found recent research on these first Africans.

"Look, Mike. Your ninth-generation grandparents are listed in some of the nation's oldest documents. Look at these old land records. This is amazing!" his mom said in astonishment.

As she read about their path to America, it became

clear those early Africans had endured many hardships. Their story was one of struggle and pain.

"Mom, I'd like to share this at our Thankful for My Family celebration next week," Mike said.

"Sure. You could relate how these early Africans survived a massacre back in their kingdom in Africa, were forced to march hundreds of miles, and then were put aboard a slave ship. Later, their ship was captured by two English pirates who eventually brought them to the English settlement of Virginia."

Mike laughed as he rubbed his forehead in amazement. "You can't make this stuff up! It's like that commercial on TV, about the truth being stranger than fiction."

His mother suggested they check out the Library of Congress website to see what they could find there. They saw maps and drawings of places, people, and events that dated back to the 1600s. The most interesting document was a list of names of people living in the settlement in 1623. Mike's ancestor's name was on it.

"Can we print this list on some paper that makes it

look old? I can put it on my display board."

"It says you can use the information for a single classroom, Mike. If you decide to do more with these resources, you need to review the copyright guidelines," his mother said. "It's important to always check the copyright restrictions for any documents you use."

"That's cool. I'm only going to use it for this school project," he said. "I think Ms. Johansson will be very impressed."

"I'm sure she will be. I know I am," his mom said, and patted him on the back. "I'm so proud of you and how you're embracing your ancestry like this. It's a wonderful gift you've received—a real treasure!"

Mike smiled and hugged his mom.

"Thanks for your help … and thanks for being my mom!"

Chapter 26 – It's the Right Thing to Do!

At the same time, at Robbie's house, his family was eating dinner. They didn't talk much. His father was usually tired and just wanted to eat.

Robbie cleared his throat and told them he had learned something cool at school that day.

"We're doing this family history project, and Ms. Johansson helped me research our family's history online." He paused.

No one said anything.

"Did you know that we have a relative who helped the colonists during the American Revolution?" he said, his voice triumphant.

More silence.

Then his father said, "You can't trust all that garbage they put on the internet."

Though he was disappointed, Robbie said, "I

discovered something else today."

Another stretch of silence.

His mother asked him what else he had learned at school.

Robbie answered, "I didn't learn it at school. I found it in the old Beulah Cemetery."

"What were you doing in the cemetery?" his father asked gruffly. "Is that what your school is doing these days? Getting kids to go to places where they shouldn't be going?"

Henry gave Robbie a dirty look. Their mother looked pale.

"I went with a friend, Manuel Martinez, who was looking for his relatives' graves. And guess what?" He charged on before anyone could answer or he lost his nerve. "I found Grandma Langford's grave."

The only sound in the room was the ticking of the kitchen clock. Everyone stared at Robbie, but no one said anything.

After putting down his knife and fork, his father said, "I don't think you need to go there. That's ancient history and should be left alone. And I don't want you hanging out with *those Mexicans.*"

He got up, left the dining room table, lumbered into the living room, and turned on the TV.

Robbie glared at his plate. Henry stirred his mashed potatoes around, and Mrs. Langford stared out the window.

"That was a stupid thing to say, Robbie," Henry said. "And even more stupid that you went there in the first place."

"It's part of our family history project that we're doing at school. Manuel wanted to find some family graves, and so Mike and I went to help him."

"Is that Maria Martinez's little brother?" Henry asked, his interest sparked.

"I guess so. I think Manuel has an older sister. Why?"

"Oh, nothing. She's in my English class," he said. "She's kinda cute."

"Well, don't let Dad hear you say that," Robbie said. "We're not supposed to hang out with those Mexicans." He tilted his head and frowned in their father's direction.

Their mother was clearing the table. Robbie followed her into the kitchen. He asked her why his father acted that way.

She said that at the time of his mother's death, his father had not seen her for more than a year.

"I think he was ashamed. He didn't even go to her funeral," Robbie's mother said. "As you can see, he doesn't like to talk about it."

"Is that why we never see Grandpa Langford anymore?"

"Yes, I'm sorry to say." She started loading the dishes into the dishwasher.

After he sat on a kitchen stool and thought about it a few minutes, he said, "You know, Mom, she's not only his mother. She's my grandmother, and I remember her. I'm going to put some flowers on her grave and I don't care what he says!"

He stormed out of the room.

Chapter 27 – Connecting with the Past

Excitement was building in the classroom as the small groups planned for their Thankful for My Family program.

Fiona and Margaret were in the group collecting photographs and artifacts. Fiona brought in more pictures of her great-grandparents, who had stayed behind in Ireland. She also did online research and found additional pictures and maps of the area where they had lived.

Margaret was creating a poster about the Tuskegee Airmen, the first African American military aviators in the US Army Air Corps. She listed many of the accomplishments that these pilots had achieved during World War II. One of the websites she read said they flew more than 1,500 combat missions.

"I'm so proud of my great-grandfather," Margaret

said. "I wish I coulda met him. My dad said he'd let me bring in some of his medals."

After he heard Margaret talking about the military, Robbie surprised the others when he spoke up and finally showed interest in the class project.

"I have a relative who was part of the American Revolution," he said. "I hope Mrs. Tucker can help me find out exactly what he did. Maybe he got medals too, although I think he was just a farmer."

"It doesn't matter if he got any medals," Fiona said. "He helped our country become independent. You should be very proud of that!"

Robbie smiled. "Yeah, I am."

The group working on clothing from different cultures discussed garments and headwear from Europe and the Middle East.

Some of the girls asked Yasmine about the head coverings worn by the women in her culture. She said she could demonstrate several different veils and coverings worn by women throughout the Muslim world. A few other girls in the class suggested she do a fashion show, and they volunteered to be models.

Yasmine was beginning to feel included.

Samuel said, "Don't forget about me. I'll wear a yarmulke."

"Are those the little beanies that Jewish men wear?" Johnny asked. "Why do they do that?"

In an enthusiastic tone, Samuel shed light on the topic. "Jewish men have worn head coverings for thousands of years. I found out there are many variations, depending on the group they belonged to. Sometimes it's called a yarmulke and sometimes a kippah. They all have a religious meaning. They are a way to honor God."

Ms. Johansson heard their discussion while she was wandering around the room. "Class, isn't it interesting that so many of these cultures have similar traditions?" she said. "It seems we have much in common."

Billy shared that he found he had a distant relative who was a member of the Lewis and Clark Expedition in the early 1800s. "They were a group of explorers who helped create maps of the land acquired west of the

Mississippi River in the Louisiana Purchase. President Thomas Jefferson was eager to find a route across the country's western part and to discover what resources were there,"Billy said."They were also trying to establish contact with the Native Americans."

"How long did it take them to make that trip?" Margaret asked.

"They left from St. Louis, Missouri, and traveled west across the country to the Pacific Ocean, ending up in Oregon. It took them about three years to go there and return,"he said."They faced many dangers, such as bad weather, but got help from Native American tribes along the way—which was kinda cool."

I bet my mom could help me make an outfit like they wore, Billy thought. *I've always wanted to wear a coonskin hat like Davy Crockett's.*

Chapter 28 – Thankful for My Family

Finally, the big day arrived. Some of the more artistic students had made invitations to send home to their parents and other family members. Because the program would take place in the afternoon right after lunch, for refreshments the students decided to include desserts and sweets from family cookbooks.

They planned to hold their program in the school auditorium, which had a stage. Many of them spent most of the morning setting up their displays and working with the media specialist to have a microphone and projector setup. Each of the students had submitted family photos for a slide presentation that would be shown to their families.

Soon, parents, grandparents, brothers, sisters, and even a few aunts and uncles arrived. Several students greeted them at the door, saying "welcome" in the language of their ancestors. Colorful banners were draped across the stage, displaying words of welcome in different languages—although they didn't seem so unfamiliar anymore to the students. Festive music from Cuba and Mexico, selected by Manuel and Walter, was playing in the background.

Manuel's parents, grandparents, and sister found seats in the front of the room because Manuel's grandfather was hard of hearing. Mike's family was also there, joined by Mike's newly-found cousin Eddie.

Robbie's mother, father, and brother sat near the back. Henry kept looking around the room and smiled at the sight of Maria Martinez and her family.

While other family members trickled in and found their seats, Robbie saw his grandfather standing at the back of the room. He walked toward him slowly at first and then started running. He gave him a big hug and thanked him for coming.

"I saved a seat for you with the rest of my family," he said.

When they approached where his family was sitting,

Robbie saw the surprise on his father's face.

"I invited Grandpa Langford," he said. "We're supposed to be celebrating our family, so I wanted my grandpa here too."

Robbie's father stood up and awkwardly said, "Hi, Dad. It's been a while."

"Yes, it has. But I'm here now, and it's good to see you." They shook hands.

Robbie's mother jumped up and hugged Grandpa Langford, and Henry did the same.

Robbie returned to the front of the room, where his classmates were seated. He had a broad grin on his face and did a fist pump in the air.

Chapter 29 – Sharing Traditions

Ms. Johansson went to the center of the stage and announced that the program was about to begin. When everyone was seated, she thanked them for coming and told them how thrilled she was with her students.

"Your kids have done a wonderful job with our little project. Not only did they master many new skills on how to do research online, but they also learned some history, geography, and about the cultures from many other countries. You should be very proud of them," she said. "And without further ado, I'm turning the program over to the students."

David walked onto the stage, carrying a violin.

"This violin belonged to my grandfather," he said. "He brought it with him from Japan when he first came to America. It's a family treasure and I don't usually get to play it. My parents have allowed me to play it for you today. I hope you like it."

He played some music composed by Ludwig van Beethoven. The rest of the students sat spellbound. They didn't know David could play the violin. He and Ms. Johansson had kept it a secret. When he had finished the piece, the students applauded enthusiastically and so did the rest of the audience. He bowed and strode with confidence from the stage.

Fiona then stepped up to the microphone. "Ladies and gentlemen, we have a special fashion show we'd like to share with you."

Billy entered the stage wearing a fur hat, a fringed buckskin jacket, and leather boots. He walked back and forth across the front of the stage and lifted an antique handheld spyglass to one of his eyes as if looking for something in the distance. Fiona announced that Billy had discovered that he had a relative who had been a part of the Lewis and Clark Expedition. Billy moved to one side of the stage.

Next, Yasmine walked shyly onto the stage. She was wearing a hijab, a scarf covering her head and neck and tied under her chin. Fiona described that Muslim women cover their hair to show their modesty and to honor their religion. Annie and Angela joined Yasmine. They were each wearing other forms of head coverings.

"In many Islamic cultures, women wear hijabs in public and remove them when they go home." Fiona gestured to the girls near her. "Head coverings are worn by women in many cultures and different religious groups to show their religious commitment."

The three girls moved to the other side of the stage from Billy.

Manuel's grandmother whispered to Maria that she had worn a lace veil on her head for her First Communion in a Catholic church in Mexico.

In a whisper, Maria replied, "It's amazing to see how many religious traditions are similar."

Next, Samuel joined his classmates on the stage.

Fiona was ready for this introduction, too. "Likewise," she said, "Jewish men show the same respect for their religion by wearing a yarmulke. It's their way to honor God. Some Orthodox Jews wear them all the time, and others wear them only at prayer times, during rituals, or when attending services at the temple."

Samuel, who was always trying to be funny, imitated a runway model by striding across the stage with one hand on his hip, turning his head from side to side, and raising his hand and pointing to the top of his head."

His classmates laughed, but his father was not amused.

The audience clapped when the students left the stage. Then the students were asked to join their families in the audience for the next part of the program.

Chapter 30 – Sharing Family Photos

Fiona turned the microphone over to Anthony.

"Next up, some photographs of our families," he said. "Emma and I created this slide presentation to show some of the things we learned from the written documents we found and the stories we heard from many of you. We think you'll see some familiar faces, and we hope you like it."

Emma started the projector. As the photos appeared on the screen, the song "I'm Proud to Be an American" began playing quietly in the background. The title slide was a photo of the world map they had used, with the red pins indicating the many places where the students had family connections.

The following slide depicted an artist's drawing of Virginia in the 1600s. A photo of Mike Murphy's biological family members at a recent reunion in Virginia was next to it. Mike's cousin beamed when he saw it.

Anthony said, "Mike Murphy discovered he was related to the first Africans brought to Virginia in 1619. They were supposed to go to Veracruz, Mexico, but were taken to Virginia instead. Mike will be connecting with many of his relatives this summer, for the first time."

Manuel's grandfather told his family, "I grew up in Veracruz! What a small world we live in."

Next, a photograph of Meriwether Lewis and William Clark was positioned next to an old map of the western United States.

Anthony said, "Lewis and Clark were explorers who headed an expedition to explore and map the newly-purchased Louisiana Territory in the early 1800s. These men were hunters and loved the outdoors."

Then a photo of Billy and his father appeared that was taken on a fishing trip. "Perhaps that's why Billy and his father like to go fishing. It's in their genes. Billy discovered he has a relative who was part of that expedition."

The next slide was of Ellis Island. Anthony remarked

that Ellis Island was a place in New York Harbor where many immigrants from Europe went through their immigration processing procedures there in the late 1800s and early 1900s. The next several slides showed black-and-white photographs of students' relatives who had first set foot on American soil there.

Samuel's father said, "There's my grandfather, shortly after he arrived from Poland."

Angela's mother clapped her hands when she recognized her great-grandmother, who was posed in a photo with her six children.

With a tear in her eye, Angela's mother said, "She crossed the Atlantic from Italy with two small children, with no help. That little girl in her lap is my grandmother, who was born several years later in this country."

Angela told her mother that she had found records showing that her great-great-grandmother first entered America at Ellis Island.

Several other group photos were shared of families gathering in front of their homes or in their living rooms. Margaret was incredibly proud of the collage of photos of her great-grandfather and the Tuskegee Airmen.

Anthony said, "Several of our class members have relatives who fought in wars, like Margaret's great-great-grandfather and Manuel's great-great-grandfather." A series of photographs of men and women in military uniforms appeared to the quiet, respectful audience.

"We even have one member who can trace his roots back to the American Revolution. Robbie Langford comes from a long line of farmers, and one of them may have left his farm to help fight the British at Lexington, in 1775. We're glad he survived, or Robbie wouldn't be here today!"

Everyone laughed.

Robbie's father stared straight ahead. "Is that correct?" he asked Robbie.

"Yeah. I worked with Mrs. Tucker, who really knows how to find these things. We also have relatives living in Massachusetts today. Did you know that?"

His father shook his head. He sat back in his chair and stared at the floor for a long time.

More photos were shared, and many comments

like "Oh, look. There's Grandpa" and "I remember that photo of my mother" could be heard around the room.

The last slide showed a group photo of the class, with a caption that read: "We're the next generation of Americans!"

Anthony said, "That concludes our presentation. Ms. Johansson would like to say a few words."

The students cheered and stood up and clapped when Ms. Johansson approached the microphone.

"Thank you so much. This has been one of the best projects I've ever undertaken in my nine years of teaching. I want to thank Mrs. Tucker, the professional genealogist who taught us how to trace our families' roots."

Mrs. Tucker stood up and nodded her head while the students cheered loudly.

Ms. Johansson said, "I'd also like to thank the parents, grandparents, and other relatives who helped provide information about their families, and for the photographs and memorabilia that you see displayed around the room."

Her gaze scanned the audience before she said, "Something very interesting happened when the students did this research about their ancestors. They discovered many new things about their families' histories—and they found they had some unexpected connections to one another.

"For example, Mike's early African ancestors were captured off a ship near Veracruz, Mexico, where Manuel's grandparents lived before coming to Florida. Emma, Fiona, Angela, and Samuel all had great-grandparents who entered the United States through Ellis Island. Billy's relative ended up near Astoria, Oregon, on the Lewis and Clark Expedition, where Emma's great-grandfather lived after he left Finland. Robbie and Fiona both had ancestors who settled in Massachusetts. Walter and Manuel shared a love of Latin music because they'd been hearing it for most of their lives. And Yasmine and Angela learned their families served similar foods, despite coming from very different cultures."

Again, she paused and looked around the room.

"We are connected in so many ways and we're all a part of that melting pot called America. At the beginning of this project, I asked the class to think about who they are. I hope they now have a better understanding of who they are, as well as who we are as a country.

"Before we bring our Thankful for My Family program to a close, I want to express my biggest thanks to my students. I am so proud of them. When we first started this project, some of them thought it was pointless to learn about people who are no longer with us. Today, I'm glad to say that each one of them has gained a new appreciation for their family, both past and present."

Chapter 31 – Families Connect

When the program was over, parents and grandparents were hugging their children.

Angela wanted her parents to meet Yasmine's parents. "Her mother makes a flatbread that is similar to the pizza crust that you make, Mom."

Mike's cousin visited with Margaret's grandfather, asking him if he'd like to come to the next family reunion in Virginia to tell them about the Tuskegee Airmen. "My uncles would love to hear about your grandfather."

Ms. Johansson told David's father that her father, who was from Sweden, also played the violin. She had never learned to play, but was so pleased that David had carried on his family tradition.

"This has been a wonderful experience for David," Mr. Ito said. "He was always embarrassed to tell his friends that he played the violin. I think today has changed that. Thank you for helping these students embrace their heritage."

When Manuel's grandfather walked toward the display tables, he made eye contact with Robbie's grandfather. They both stood there for a long moment, staring at each other.

Robbie's grandfather said, "Eduardo, is that you?"

"*Si, amigo.*"

The two men suddenly embraced, and then, at arm's length, stared at each other for another long minute.

"Grandpa," Robbie said. "What's going on?"

"This is my old friend, Eduardo. We worked together in the orange groves for many years," he said. "None of you would be here today if it wasn't for him."

Robbie's father, standing nearby, said, "What are you talking about?"

"Eduardo saved my life. One night, it was freezing, and we were placing smudge pots between the orange trees to keep them from freezing. One of the pots tipped over on top of my legs. Eduardo saw it happen and immediately carried me to the workstation. He saw that I could not walk.

"Fortunately, our foreman was close by. He rushed me to the hospital in his truck," Robbie's grandfather said. "Because of Eduardo's quick action, the doctors were able to treat me. That prevented serious infection. Otherwise, I might not be here. I had to stay in the hospital for many days."

He pulled up one of his pant legs and showed them the scars on his leg from the burns. "Eduardo probably saved my life that night."

Robbie's father reached out his hand to Eduardo. "Thank you for doing that," he said in a strong, warm tone of voice.

"*De nada,*" Eduardo said. "Your father and I were *amigos*."

The two older men found chairs where they could sit and visit.

Henry had been listening to this and noticed that Maria had also heard the story.

"Well, I guess this kinda makes us related," Henry said.

"I don't think so," she said with a grin. "It does show that we have some shared history. Isn't that what this project is about?"

"Yeah, you're right," he said. "And you were right about another thing."

"What's that?" she asked.

He pulled a paperback copy of *Animal Farm* out of his back pocket. "There is more to this story than a bunch of farm animals."

She laughed. "I'm glad I was able to enlighten you."

"Now that we're friends, can I call you sometime? I don't think your father will object anymore."

"Sure," she said. "And when you call me, ask for Pinky." She spun around and walked away.

Henry stood there, looking confused.

Manuel said, "You might want to take her out for breakfast. She really likes eggs."

Henry still looked puzzled. Then it dawned on him what it meant. He shook his head, grinning from ear to ear, and went to join his parents.

Chapter 32 – Thanksgiving

On Thanksgiving Day, Grandpa Langford joined Robbie and his family for dinner. He brought two bouquets of flowers.

"This one is for my daughter-in-law, who I remember is a wonderful cook."

"Who's the other one for?" Robbie asked.

"They're for your grandmother. I'm going to visit her grave later today."

"Can I go with you?" Robbie asked.

"I would like that," he said.

After a delicious turkey dinner with all the trimmings, Robbie's father and grandfather sat on the back porch. Sometimes they talked and sometimes they sat there quietly.

* * *

At Mike's house, the discussion at the dinner table

centered around their plans for a summer trip. Mike's cousin Eddie had invited the whole family to attend his next family reunion in Virginia.

"I have a feeling you'll be quite the center of attention," Sarah said. "Who knew my little brother was related to such significant ancestors!"

"Hey, Mom," Danny said, "can we check our family roots to see how far back our ancestors can be traced?"

"I'm already on it," she replied. "I wouldn't be surprised if we could connect your dad's family to Mike's biological family. He has relatives throughout the South."

They were thoughtful for a few minutes.

Then Mike said, "I'm really glad Ms. Johansson had us do this project. Not only for me, but for all the kids. It's been cool to see the different connections we have to each other."

Chapter 33 – What's Next?

On the first day back to school after the Thanksgiving break, things in the fifth-grade classroom had returned to normal. Throughout the morning, the students worked on math problems, answered questions about the solar system during their science lesson, and shared thoughts on global warming during a current events discussion.

"Ms. Johansson, what are we going to do for our next project?" Anthony asked. "Searching our family histories was fun!"

Many of the other students agreed.

Fiona said, "We want to *do* something real, not just read about it in books or online."

"What do you suggest, class?" Ms. Johansson said.

No one said anything … until Manuel said he had an idea.

"When I visited the cemetery where my grandmother is buried, I noticed that many of the graves were in pretty bad shape."

"Yeah, weeds were growing everywhere, and many of the headstones could use a good cleaning," Mike added. "Maybe we could do something about that."

Some of his classmates seemed excited about it, but some were not.

One student called out, "Cemeteries are creepy!"

Ms. Johansson told them that cemeteries are special places, and there are rules and regulations about how they should be maintained.

"Why don't I ask Mrs. Tucker to come to talk to us so we can learn more about it? I think she's certified in cemetery preservation and restoration."

Two days later, Mrs. Tucker visited the class again. Her handouts for the class listed the rules for cleaning and restoring cemeteries. As she read over the handout, she gave details about the different types of headstones and the cleaning ingredients which bring them back to life.

In conclusion, she said, "Cemeteries are significant to genealogy. If you get the chance to visit or clean up a cemetery, you should notice everything on the headstones. The dates, their names, even symbols you may see. They're all pieces of that person's puzzle. Clues about their life."

"I didn't know anything about properly cleaning up an old cemetery," Manuel whispered to Robbie.

"It sounds important," Mike said.

"It's a big responsibility," Robbie said. "I need to make sure Grandma Langford's grave is taken care of. I don't want Grandpa to see it looking rundown."

When Mrs. Tucker was finished, Manuel said he thought their class should make it their next class project—to do a cleanup day at the cemetery. He said, "We could do it on a Saturday and get our families involved."

Several other students liked that idea.

Fiona said, "Mrs. Tucker, would you be willing to help us do this, and make sure we do everything right?"

"I'd be delighted," she said. "I can apply for any

necessary permits, and I can ask the local historical society to help with the proper cleaning supplies. I'll let Ms. Johansson identify a date and she will have to communicate with each of your parents."

After Mrs. Tucker left, Ms. Johansson asked the students if this was something they wanted to do. "If you're not comfortable doing this, you don't have to participate."

Robbie asked, "Are we gonna get a grade for this?"

Ms. Johansson said there would be no grades. It would be a volunteer project that would happen on a Saturday.

Fiona said, "That's what I meant when I said we needed to *do* something, not just read or talk about it. I'm excited!"

Chapter 34
Cemeteries Are About Remembering

On the Saturday before their Christmas vacation began, twenty-one students, twenty-seven adults, Ms. Johansson, and Mrs. Tucker arrived at the Beulah Cemetery at 9:00 a.m. Mrs. Tucker brought buckets, different kinds of scrub brushes, a hose, and the cleaning liquid she had described to the class. The students brought hoes, rakes, and grass clippers with them, as Mrs. Tucker had instructed.

Manuel's mother had coordinated with some of the other parents to bring snacks and drinks. Samuel's father had arranged for a local fast-food restaurant to provide lunch for everyone, and he volunteered to pick it up at noon.

Mrs. Tucker gave instructions on what she called "best practices." First, they should remove fallen limbs, leaves, and debris. Then they would identify the locations of the headstones, footstones, monuments, and tributes left by visitors. Once they had identified the graves, it was time for the cleanup.

Soon the cemetery was busy with activity. A local news reporter showed up with a photographer to do a story. She asked Ms. Johansson why the students had become interested in a cemetery.

"It started with a project about their family histories," she said. "The students learned a great deal about their ancestors and how they became a part of our country. Cleaning up this cemetery became a way for them to show their appreciation and respect for those who came before them. And some of them even have relatives buried here."

The reporter walked around, asking questions to many of the students. She stopped where Manuel had placed a bunch of pink carnations in a vase on his great-grandmother's grave. He told the reporter that he had never met his great-grandmother, but after learning more about her he felt connected to her.

"I'm sure it was hard for her when she first came here from Mexico," he said while he arranged the flowers. "She didn't even speak English. I'm proud of her. My grandmother tells me pink was my great-grandmother's favorite color."

The photographer took a picture of Manuel standing by the grave with his grandparents.

Robbie's family, including his father and grandfather, trimmed the overgrown grass around his grandmother's grave. His grandfather had already scrubbed some of the dirt and mold off the headstone.

"Here, Dad, let me help with that," Robbie's father said.

He and Robbie's grandfather worked silently side by side.

Robbie's mother put an arm around Robbie and whispered, "Thank you for making this happen."

When they were finished, Robbie and his grandfather placed a fresh bouquet of flowers on her grave.

Shortly after noon, Samuel's dad arrived with chicken nuggets for the kids and sandwiches for the adults. Manuel's mom and Robbie's mom made sure everyone had something to drink and distributed homemade oatmeal cookies. Robbie grinned when he saw the cookies that he knew were made with his grandmother's recipe.

"These are delicious," Mrs. Martinez said. "May I have the recipe? My mother used to make some just like this."

During the lunch break, the kids gathered in a section by themselves, wanting to spend time with their classmates. The parents and other adults found cooling shade under a huge oak tree and compared their aches and pains. However, none of them were complaining. They agreed they enjoyed what they were doing.

"I want to take a group photo," Ms. Johansson said. "I plan to take a picture of what it looks like when we finish. I took pictures earlier this morning, before we started, so we can compare the before and after."

The group gathered around the entrance to the cemetery for the photo. Parents, grandparents, family members, and students wore big smiles on their faces, reflecting how they felt for what they were doing.

Afterward, they wandered back to various parts of the cemetery to continue the cleanup. Ms. Johansson took more pictures of them working and proudly watched the flurry of activity around her.

Fiona, Margaret, and Yasmine giggled about something while they pulled weeds in a family plot.

It's nice to see Yasmine laughing, Ms. Johansson thought.

Manuel's father was struggling to move a large limb that had fallen and was covering several graves. Robbie's father rushed over to help him.

Maria Martinez was busy raking up leaves and grass clippings. Henry Langford strolled over with a garbage bag and offered to help. She smiled up at him, and soon they were stuffing garbage bags as a team.

On the far side of the cemetery, Samuel and his father placed small stones on some of the headstones. This Jewish tradition was a way of honoring the dead.

When the sun dropped behind the trees and the air felt chilly, Mrs. Tucker told them it was time to wrap it up.

"I think we've done enough for today," Mrs. Tucker

said. "You've made a big difference here. It looks much better."

"Can we do this again?" Johnny asked.

"That's up to you students," Ms. Johansson said. "I hope these projects have helped you understand who we are as a country. And even though our ancestors come from many different parts of the world, I think you've discovered that we're more alike than we are different."

Many of the parents were nodding their heads in agreement. New friendships had been formed and old friends had reconnected. Families had learned many new things about their ancestors and sometimes about each other.

Before they left, Mrs. Tucker thanked them and said, "Many of the people buried here and in cemeteries across the United States came here from other countries. And yet, they're buried on American soil. Cemeteries are about remembering. We must always honor their memory, like you've done here today."

"And it's important that we remember their stories,"

Mike's mother added.

Ms. Johansson looked at her students and thought, *I wonder what their stories will be?*

Acknowledgments

As coauthors of this book, we owe a debt of gratitude to the numerous individuals who offered feedback on the material we included on the many historic topics we shared with our young readers. We communicated with individuals at the Statue of Liberty National Monument and Ellis Island Research Library, the Lewis and Clark National Historic Trail Interpretive Center, the Trail of Tears National Historic Trail, the National Underground Railroad Network to Freedom, the Afro-American Historical and Genealogical Society, the Fort Mose Historical Society, and the US National Park Service Tuskegee Airmen National Historic Site.

We could not have created this book without the expertise of numerous publishing professionals, including our developmental editor, Ericka McIntyre; our copyeditor, Beth Mansbridge; our book designer, Elizabeth Blacker; and our cover designer, Mike

Woodcock. Our heartfelt thanks go to them for their advice and support.

We also want to express our appreciation to the numerous beta readers who took the time to read our manuscript and offer comments that made our story so much better.

We are especially grateful to our husbands, Tom Knight and Terry Wood, who are constant sources of support, encouragement, and patience. We couldn't do it without them.

Other Books by K. I. Knight

"Fate & Freedom – Book I, The Middle Passage" reveals the story of two African children, Margaret and John, captured and shipped away to their doom in the silver mines of Mexico. But before the slaver can reach its destination, the ship is pirated and their new destination becomes a small English settlement in the New World. The year is 1619.

2020 Independent Publisher's Book Awards – Best Series

"Fate & Freedom – Book II, The Turning Tides" The saga continues… From Merchant's Row on the shores of the James River to the twisted truths on the high seas, Margaret and John learn to navigate the rough waters of the first English Colony of Virginia.

2020 Independent Publisher's Book Awards – Best Series

"Fate & Freedom – Book III, On Troubled Shores" The conclusion of the epic saga will leave you holding your breath right up until the very end. The shores of the James River are eroding rapidly as Margaret and John struggle to remain afloat and retain the simplest of freedoms to escape slavery during the earliest years of America's birth.

2020 Independent Publisher's Book Awards – Best Series

"UNVEILED – The Twenty & Odd" reveals the true story of the landing of the first Africans in England's America. For the first time, America will understand who these first Africans were, from where they came, the struggles they faced, and the amazing achievements they made.

2019 Phyllis Wheatley Literacy Award

2020 Independent Publisher's Book Awards – Research

Books available at
www.firstfreedompublishing.com

Other Books by Jane R. Wood

Voices in St. Augustine
Thirteen-year-old Joey Johnson has a problem. He hears voices, only he can't find the people who belong to them. His curiosity leads him on a quest where he learns more than just history about the Nation's Oldest City.

Mom's Choice Awards® Silver Recipient

Adventures on Amelia Island:
A Pirate, a Princess, and Buried Treasure
This book continues the escapades of the Johnson family. Local legends and tales of ghosts add to a story filled with colorful characters, humorous situations, and a youthful spirit of adventure.

Mom's Choice Awards® Silver Recipient

Trouble on the St. Johns River
After a close encounter with a manatee, a visit to a sea turtle center, and a family river tour, Joey, Bobby, and Katy decide to "do something" to try to make a difference in protecting endangered animals and preserving the environment.

Mom's Choice Awards® Silver Recipient

Ghosts on the Coast: A Visit to Savannah
and the Low Country
It seems wherever they go, adventure follows the Johnson family. This time it comes when they visit the historic cities of Savannah, Charleston, and Pawleys Island, South Carolina—cities rich in history and ghost stories!

Mom's Choice Awards® Silver Recipient

Lost in Boston
In *Lost in Boston,* the Johnson family tours several historic landmarks in Boston, including the Paul Revere House, the Old North Church, and the USS *Constitution.* Riding a subway for the first time, sampling new foods, and solving a crime add discovery and intrigue to this newest family adventure.

Mom's Choice Awards® Silver Recipient

All of Jane R. Wood's books may be ordered through
www.janewoodbooks.com

About the Coauthors

Kathryn Knight, who uses the pen name *K. I. Knight,* is an international award-winning author, genetic genealogist, American historian, keynote speaker, and cemetery preservationist. For over thirteen years, Knight documented more than 20,000 hours researching the first recorded Africans to arrive in the English settlement of Virginia in 1619. Her passion is unrivaled and strongly evident in her published writings. Her literary works include *Fate & Freedom*, a five-star Gold medal historical trilogy detailing the lives of the 1619 Africans, as well as her nonfiction work, *Unveiled – The Twenty & Odd: Documenting the First Africans in England's America 1619–1625 and Beyond*, for which she was awarded the Phillis Wheatley Book Award by the Sons and Daughters of the US Middle Passage. Knight is a board member for several national nonprofit organizations and a member of numerous genealogical, historical, and literary societies. The mother of three adult children, the author lives in North Florida with her husband, Tom.

 ***Jane R. Wood*** is the author of five award-winning juvenile fiction books in which she weaves history and science into stories of mystery, adventure, and humor for young readers, ages 8–14. Students like her books because they're fun—teachers like them for their educational value. Wood is a former teacher, newspaper reporter, and television producer. She has a BA from the University of Florida and an MEd from the University of North Florida. Wood has served in leadership positions on several nonprofit boards involved in education, international relations, and book publishing. The author lives in Jacksonville, Florida, with her husband, Terry, and is the mother of two grown sons and five grandchildren. To learn more about her and her books, please visit her website at janewoodbooks.com.